PUFFIN

Editor: Kaye Webb

NO MORE SCHOOL

'No more school,' Miss Oldroyd announced. 'Not for a week, anyway,' and she closed the door of the school, turned the key in the lock, pulled it out, and hung it in its little place in the wall.

But at the end of the week there was a message that Miss Oldroyd was ill, and wouldn't be back for a fortnight.

So they had to go to Burton school instead; Ruth said she'd show them. 'That road's much twistier than you think,' she said. 'It goes miles and miles round, so you're always miles and miles off Burton, and when you've got to Burton you're still miles and miles off Burton school.' And then in the end she brought them to their own school.

She put her hand in the hole in the wall and brought out the key. She put it in the lock, turned it, lifted the latch, and pushed the door open.

'Come on,' she said. 'Time for lessons to begin.'

This nice, funny, original book is for readers of eight upwards. The other books by William Mayne, published in Puffins, are *Earthfasts*, *A Book of Heroes*, *Ravensgill*, *A Book of Giants*, *Royal Harry* and *A Game of Dark*.

No More School

WILLIAM MAYNE

Illustrated by Peter Warner

PUFFIN BOOKS

Puffin Books: a Division of Penguin Books Ltd, Harmondsworth, Middlesex, England
Penguin Books Australia Ltd, Ringwood, Victoria, Australia
Penguin Books Canada Ltd, 41 Steelcase Road West, Markham, Ontario, Canada
Penguin Books (N.Z.) Ltd, 182-190 Wairau Road, Auckland 10, New Zealand

—

First published by Hamish Hamilton 1965
Published in Puffin Books 1968
Reprinted 1970, 1972, 1975

—

Copyright © William Mayne, 1965
Illustrations © Peter Warner, 1965

—

Made and printed in Great Britain
by Hazell Watson & Viney Ltd
Aylesbury, Bucks
Set in Linotype Baskerville

Chapter One

'No more school,' said Miss Oldroyd. She closed the door of the school kitchen and picked up the board rubber, which had fallen off its ledge again and left a chalky mark on the floor. 'No more school,' she said again. 'Not for a week, anyway. But don't forget to come back on Monday.'

'The Monday after next,' said Ruth.

'Not next Monday, no,' said Miss Oldroyd. 'I have to have a holiday as well. Now let's stand up and have prayers.'

After prayers Ruth opened the door, because she was nearer to it than Shirley was. Bobby came to the door as well, to hold it open, though it would stay open very well by itself. He was not really holding it open, but waiting for Miss Oldroyd to remember something.

She did remember. 'Somebody's turn for a lift,' she said. 'Bobby, I think.'

Bobby stood on his toes, and then down on his heels again, because he was glad that she had remembered.

'We'll go last, Bobby,' said Miss Oldroyd. 'But we shall get there first.'

They waited in the porch until all the others had got out of school. Miss Oldroyd looked into the boys' cloak-

room and then the girls' cloakroom to see that no taps
were left running, and that no coats had been left
behind. No one was wearing coats today, because of
the fine weather, but they still might have brought
them. They did not want to have the coats locked in
the school for two week-ends and the whole week
between.

'That's all,' said Miss Oldroyd, giving the drinking
water filter's tap a last turn to make sure. 'Let's go,
Bobby.'

She closed the door of the school, turned the key
in the lock, pulled the key out, and hung it in its
little place in the wall. It rang a little note as it
swung.

Her car was a very small one. It was big enough for
two people, but they could not sit side by side. They
had to sit one behind the other, with the driver in
front, of course. Bobby got in first.

'You're facing the wrong way,' said Miss Oldroyd.
'But I suppose you're better that way round. If you
face the front you only see my back.'

'I can look out of the back window,' said Bobby. 'I'll tell you if anyone comes racing up to us.'

Miss Oldroyd got in. The little car rocked about. She closed the door and pulled down the window. She turned on the petrol and waited for it to get to the engine. Then she started the engine. Blue smoke curled all round the car and came in at the window.

Miss Oldroyd made her racing start. The engine went very fast, and then slowed down, because they had begun to climb a hill.

'Push hard,' said Miss Oldroyd. Bobby laughed, and pushed on the back of the seat, until he thought he was really pushing the wrong way. Of course, it would make no difference how ever much he pushed.

They chugged up the hill. Bobby watched the trees coming into sight from behind him. Miss Oldroyd sounded the horn, and they went past the infants. All five of them waved, and pointed at Bobby. The car passed the rest of the school.

'Five infants,' said Miss Oldroyd. 'Seven big ones, and you, that makes thirteen. There's one more.'

'It's Fletcher,' said Bobby. 'He went down to the hayfield to see whether they were mowing yet.'

'That's fourteen,' said Miss Oldroyd. There were only fourteen scholars in the whole school. Miss Oldroyd thought it was a nice number, two each of five, six, seven and ten, and three each of eight and nine.

The car had started last. It came to the village first. Miss Oldroyd stopped at her door, and Bobby got out. Miss Oldroyd had to get out first.

'There now,' she said, 'the motor's stopped. We'll just push it into the garden, Bobby.'

'I pushed it all the way up here,' said Bobby. 'I'll get at the back again.'

'Good,' said Miss Oldroyd. 'I forgot to put the brake on, I think, and it wants to run away down the hill again. No, I did put the brake on, but when we got out the brake let go again. I usually put a rock against the wheel, and then it can't escape.'

The car was in the garden, leaning on a stone, by the time the rest of the school had come back home.

'You sat the wrong way round,' said Shirley.

'He couldn't,' said Ruth. 'There isn't room to. I think he just took his head off and put it on the other way.'

'Like an owl,' said Miss Oldroyd. 'They can put their heads on backwards, but they don't need to take them off first.'

'It was a new way of travelling,' said Bobby. 'And when we stopped, all the things that had been going away started to look as if they were coming back again towards me. All those trees began to creep up again.'

Ruth and Shirley had a look at the trees down the road, but they had stopped creeping up again. Shirley said she didn't believe they had ever moved at all.

'It was only how it looked,' said Bobby. But Shirley would not believe it at all. Ruth walked backwards up the road, to see whether it happened to her, but all that happened was that a stinging nettle crept up on the other side of her and nipped the back of her knee. She gave up the experiment and looked for a dock leaf.

After tea Miss Oldroyd went off for her week's

holiday. She filled the back of her car with one suitcase and a floppy bag, and tried a racing start out of her gateway. It was not a good start, however, because the rock was still in front of the wheel. Bobby was on the green with Fletcher and he knew what had happened when the engine stopped. He went to take the rock away. Miss Oldroyd made her racing start, and buzzed down the hill.

'She's off,' said Fletcher. 'What'll we do for a week?'

'Rowk about,' said Bobby. 'Get in the hayfield.'

'If they cut the grass we will,' said Fletcher. 'But they aren't on with it yet.'

The next day was Saturday, and it began to rain before the daylight came, and it rained all day. It was a good thing no coats had been left in school.

'My dad says a bit of rain just now is a good thing,' said Fletcher.

He was standing by the shop turning the water at the edge of the road into a pond by putting his feet across it. He was wearing plimsolls, and the water soaked through the canvas, and then trickled in at the lace holes, and at last came in over the top. Ruth was looking in at the shop window and wondering whether to buy one length of Spanish, two sherbet dabs, three aniseed balls, or four fruity chews with one penny. In between thinking she dropped twigs into Fletcher's pond.

'Some people are funny people,' she said. 'Let it rain in winter, and have done. It needn't rain this week.'

But it did rain this week. It rained every day, though not all day. The grass never dried out, even if the sun did shine. The farmers went each day to look at the

hayfields, and were quite patient, because the grass was still growing and the rain was doing it good.

Shirley and Ruth went to market with their mothers on Friday, and it was so wet that when the bus door opened a trickle of water ran down the step. All the water was rain that had dripped from people's clothes as they sat in the bus.

'I wish we could play out,' said Ruth, on Sunday. 'When we've got to go to school tomorrow. You know, it'll stop raining as soon as we get in that door. You know weather.'

On Sunday evening, though, a message came to the shop. Fletcher heard it first, and sent it on to Bobby, who gave it to Ruth, who told Shirley's mother, because Shirley was down with Mary. Then a little later Betty looked out of her bedroom window and told Ruth.

'I know,' said Ruth. 'Miss Oldroyd's ill, and she won't be back for a fortnight.'

'Isn't it sad?' said Betty. 'I'm writing her a letter.'

Chapter Two

IN the morning, there was no hurry to get up, because there was no school to go to, in spite of the day being Monday. Ruth got out of bed when she woke up, and looked out of the window, to see what kind of day Monday was being. It was raining. She went back to bed, because there was no one outside at all. The village was empty, both the street and the green.

Later on she got up again, and shouted at the top of the stairs for breakfast. Mum looked up from the kitchen door and said it was washday, never mind the weather, and she wasn't carrying trays about. Ruth went back to bed, but the bed wasn't the same, and the pillow was tepid. She got out for the third time and looked from the window.

There were two little people in the road, mackin-toshed from ears to ankles. One was red and the other the blackish-blue you might call the natural colour of raincoats. The red one was Susan, and the blue one was Bill. They were wellingtoning on the edge of the road. Ruth could hear the ridged soles of the boots picking up the gravel and drawing it through the water.

When Ruth had come down and had breakfast, and gone to the door to look out, in case Shirley happened to be about, the two little people were still there. The red mackintosh had lost its brightness and gone drab. The blue-black one looked as if it had always been made of paper. Susan and Bill were still at the edge of the road, paddling.

Ruth put her camel coat over her head, because the camel coat hung nearest the door, and went outside. The rain began to drop on her and to stay in the wool. She thought she could feel the coat getting heavier and heavier with water. She pulled the gate open with her foot, and the water that had hung on it jumped off and ran into her sandal.

'Hello,' she said, to Bill and Susan. 'What are you doing?'

'Waiting for you,' said Susan. 'Are you off?'

'I'm off to see Shirley,' said Ruth. 'You don't want to come, you know.'

'We'll wait on,' said Bill. 'You'll not be so long, will you?'

'I might be all day,' said Ruth. 'You'll get wet, stood there.'

'Not any more,' said Bill. 'We's wet now.'

'When you come back we'll still be here,' said Susan. 'We won't be late.'

Bill and Susan had only just come past their fifth birthdays. Ruth knew what they were waiting for, and why they were standing in the road. They wanted to start school.

'Oh,' she said, 'but Miss Oldroyd's away. She's badly. Didn't you know?'

'Mum said I didn't have to go to school,' said Bill. 'But I wanted to, with all the other kids.'

'There isn't any school today,' said Ruth.

'My Mum said I'd to wait,' said Susan. 'So I am waiting. I'm waiting with Bill. I don't like Bill.'

'Your Mum will play pop with you, getting wet like that,' said Ruth. 'Go on home, you soft things, and get dried.'

'We want to go to school,' said Susan. 'They have games there. We don't have games with Bill at home. He doesn't live at my house.'

'I'm going playing,' said Ruth. 'You go home.'

Shirley was sitting in front of an empty fireplace, listening to the drops of rain as they fell down the chimney and rustled on the bare bars of the grate. There was a green light in the room from the green bushes of their garden.

'What are you doing?' said Ruth. 'I'm not doing a thing.'

'So am I not doing a thing,' said Shirley. She put out one foot and pushed something further under the settee. 'I'm bored,' she said. 'I've got up, and here I am. But I'm glad it's not school. I'm just waiting for something to happen. It might you know. Things do happen.'

'It might stop raining,' said Ruth. 'We could do something until then, and then do something else.'

'But it might not stop all day,' said Shirley. 'We might be on with the first thing all day, and that's boring, you know, because we don't want to do it now, do we?'

'I don't know what it is,' said Ruth.

In the end they pulled out the things that were under the settee. They were Shirley's dolls, which she thought she ought to give up, but didn't want to. Now she would only play with them if she thought she was pleasing Ruth. Ruth liked dolls, and thought she could go on playing with them as long as she lived. They put them on the settee instead of under it, and began to teach school. The dolls were good at being pupils, because if they started to get out of hand the teacher only had to change her mind about what the doll was saying or doing, and the doll was doing or saying something quite different.

They were quite busy when the front door opened and closed, then opened and closed again.

'Somebody's come in and gone out again,' said Shirley.

It was not quite that, though. The first opening had been Bill creeping into the house, and the second opening had been Susan creeping in. They had not come in together because they were not really friends at all.

'What are you doing?' said Bill.

'School,' said Shirley. 'Go away.'

'It's dolls,' said Susan. 'I'll play.'

'It isn't dolls,' said Shirley. 'You go away too. It isn't for little kids, and you're making the floor as wet as the fire.'

'That wouldn't matter,' said Ruth.

'Look in our fire,' said Shirley. 'It's a rain-gauge. If it was alight it'd be out.'

Ruth pulled Bill's helmet off his head. He had been out in the rain so long that she had to dry his hair as well. Shirley brought a towel to do it, because they were all in her house. Bill's head shook about as if it had not been quite fixed on when he got it.

Susan wanted hers shaken in the same way, but she had a red hood to her red coat, and the water had not come through. Bill stood and rolled his head and blinked.

'There's too many flipping kids,' said Shirley. 'This is a house, not a museum.'

'It's a zoo, I think,' said Ruth, looking at the dolls,

which were, four human, one rabbit, one monkey, one bear, one Chinese cluck, or duck, a golliwog, a clothes-peg, and a thing made out of two toffee tins and some felt but never finished, because the teacher before Miss Oldroyd had never got to the end of making it before leaving. Ruth had a blouse with one paper sleeve and one cloth one, left from the same teacher.

'It is a bit of a zoo,' said Shirley. 'There's a monkey, too, but he's watching the dairy. If we take him away he'll die because his stuffing comes out of the rat holes. It might be a catching disease.'

Bill pulled off his coat and let it lie in its own rainy juice. Susan took hers off and laid it carefully on a chair, with the dry side out so that it would not make anyone wet.

Shirley's mother found the wet chair later on and looked all over the ceiling for the place where the rain came in, not knowing that it had walked in at the front door.

Ruth moved the dolls up and put the two little children at the bottom of the class. The dolls could write, but Bill and Susan had to be taught. They still knew nothing at dinner-time, but Shirley said there was no more school for the rest of the day, and put the dolls back under the settee.

'I'll go and see if my old mum's finished washing the clobber,' said Ruth. 'I know her, she'll have it hung out, drying or something.'

It was evening when they met again. The rain had stopped, but the clouds were close to the roofs and lapping the hills. The night was growing dark early.

'Do you know,' said Shirley. 'We might have to go to Burton school. They don't like us to have holidays.'

'What's wrong with our school?' said Ruth.

'Nothing,' said Shirley. 'It's beautiful. It's closed down.'

Chapter Three

'How do you spell Bill's name?' said Shirley, the next morning.

'B, I, L, L,' said Ruth. 'Buh, Ih, Luh, Luh.'

'That's how I've done it,' said Shirley. 'But it looks wrong. It's a stupid word. I don't think I'll write to Miss Oldroyd after all. She's probably too ill to read it, and if she can she'll blow her top at my spelling. She always goes hairless if I make mistakes. I'll throw the letter away.'

Ruth had a look at the word that appeared wrong. 'You've spelt it right,' she said. 'You have to put a capital letter, that's all. Capital B.'

'You would choose something right inside the word,' said Shirley. 'I shall have to start writing it all from the beginning again, with "Dear Miss Oldroyd".'

They were outdoors today, because during the night the rain had stopped, and the sky had opened up distant and blue. The morning sun had licked up the wet from the roads and roofs, and was heating the fields so that they steamed gently. Up and down the village tractors were setting out to mow the grass for hay, each carrying a cocked-up crocodile jaw, which was the cutter bar. The smell of the grass sap was hanging in the still air like the smell of honey, and the tractors buzzed like distant bees.

Ruth and Shirley were lying in the sun on a milk stand, where the big cans were stood for collection. The milk bus had been and gone, and the cans were empty ones. Ruth was lying on the top of the cans, and Shirley on the stand itself.

'Here he comes,' said Shirley, looking out up the road. She was lying one way, and Ruth the other. Ruth turned her head and saw Bill coming down the road. She dropped off the cans, out of sight. They did not feel like playing with Bill.

Bill saw them quite well, though. Ruth thought that little people did not see so much as big ones, and lay there pretending to be a sack, rolled up with a string round its waist. Shirley shut her eyes and pretended she was not there at all. Bill came and looked at one of them, then went round the stand and looked at the other. Then he said he was going shopping, and went on with his shopping bag trailing behind him, talking to himself.

'What shall I write next?' said Shirley. 'When I wrote Bill he came along.'

'Write Susan,' said Ruth. 'Big Suh, Uh, Suh, Ah, Nuh.'

Shirley wrote it in, after Bill. 'I can't send this letter, anyway,' she said. 'It's gone strange.'

Bill came back from the shop. He was being followed by a fly, and kept swinging his shopping at it. A packet of suet fell out.

'Did you write "Fly"?' said Ruth.

'No,' said Shirley. 'I wrote Susan. Here she comes.'

Susan came down the road on her tricycle. Bill tried to take it away from her, but she went round him, and then past the milk stand, and round the corner.

'It works,' said Ruth. 'Now write Santa Claus. Let's have somebody useful we can get things from and don't have to pay, because I haven't any money.'

Shirley wrote 'Santa Claus'. No one came. Ruth climbed back on the milk cans. They were warming in the sun.

The next person to come along was Shirley's father. He had come back from the field for a rake and somebody to do the raking. Shirley went with him, to rake the newly cut grass off the cutter bar, because it was so soft and plentiful that it was choking the rattling blade.

'It's the way you spell, I think,' said Ruth, when she was walking beside Shirley, trailing a rake in the road. 'Look what you've lodged us into.'

The letter was never finished. When they came back to the milk stand the paper had gone, tugged away by some summer breeze or chased behind a wall by a cat, or perhaps made into a dart by one of the boys.

'Probably Fletcher,' said Shirley. 'We shall know, if we see a blue dart.'

They were in the field again in the afternoon, and when they came back to Shirley's house for tea, and washed their hands, they found slack blisters growing on their palms. The blisters had no feeling on their outsides, but if they pressed them they could feel the edges trying to grow larger. Shirley tried to push one blister into the next and make a long one, but all she did was burst one, and that made it sting.

'There,' she said. 'No more work for me. That's an empty cushion.'

'It's a wound,' said Ruth. 'You want something on it for cuts, wounds and stings.'

'It's only one of them,' said Shirley. But by the time they had dabbed the wound with the yellow stuff from the bottle it was two of the things, a wound and a sting. Shirley had to go and sit down and look at her tea for a long time before eating it.

In the evening Fletcher and Bobby came to lounge on the garden wall. Fletcher fell off the wall into the hedge and had to be lifted out the way he had come, so that the hedge would not be broken down. He sat on the wall again to pull the twigs out of himself.

'If it's cut, we'll put something on it,' said Ruth. 'Just look carefully.'

'You don't want to get some tree disease,' said Shirley.

'I've only got greenfly,' said Fletcher.

'We've got blisters,' said Shirley.

Bobby was envious of the blisters, but Fletcher said he had grown out of them, because his hands were hard with work all the year round.

'Is it right we've to go to Burton school?' said Bobby.

'They said so yesterday,' said Ruth. 'Some people only went to one school in their whole life. My father went to our school all his.'

'One school's enough,' said Fletcher. 'One school's plenty. We can wait for Miss Oldroyd. She won't be ill so long, I doubt.'

'We're ill more than she is,' said Bobby. 'I am, I know. I've been away more than she has, and I haven't

been off all this term, so she can't be very bad, or I'd be worse.'

'You only get schoolitis,' said Ruth. 'That's not an illness, it's an opinion.'

'I'm bad with it,' said Bobby. 'I'd be worse at Burton.'

'It's the law,' said Shirley. 'Kids have to go to school. Fancy kids having to obey the law. Kids oughtn't to have to obey the law.'

'Fancy Bill and Susan having to obey the law, when they can't even read it,' said Ruth. 'No one can read at five, so how could they know they'd got to go to school.'

'My dad says you've got to go to the nearest school,' said Fletcher. 'Burton isn't the nearest one.'

Bobby agreed with Fletcher that if the law said you had to go to the nearest school, then they had to go to their own, and if there wasn't a teacher there must be a law that said there had to be one.

'You can't have a school without a teacher,' said Ruth. 'Even dolls have to have a teacher.'

'Even kittens do,' said Shirley. 'Their mother teaches them how to drink milk and chase string, and purr, and that.'

'The teacher at Burton might not know how to teach all things like that,' said Ruth. She did not particularly mean chasing string and purring.

'It hasn't been proved,' said Shirley.

'They don't know much in Burton,' said Fletcher. 'Burton's where they think the pigs can fly to market.'

'That's it,' said Bobby. 'Burton's where they shear the sheep and throw the fleeces in the beck.'

'That's true,' said Fletcher. 'We don't want to learn all that. We'd be no good after.'

'We won't go,' said Ruth. 'We'll have a school nearer than that, in our shippon, until Miss Oldroyd gets back.'

Chapter Four

WEDNESDAY morning was a cool starter, and there was a mist hanging on the fields in the valley bottom. Ruth woke up to hear her mother shouting up that she was off to the fields, and Ruth's breakfast was on the table. Ruth got up on her elbows, and then sank down again. She thought she heard the door close, but still someone was moving about downstairs. It sounded as if the table was still in the middle of being set for breakfast. There was a smell of bacon.

Ruth got up. She put on her red jeans, red socks, and the red pullover, and put a red band round her head. She looked in the drawer and found a red handkerchief, and under the bed for her red shoes. Now she was what her mother called 'reddy'.

She went downstairs, and found the cat had gone with the bacon, and was going with the butter. She chased it out, smelt the bacon plate, and looked round for something else to eat.

She was drinking Cherry-O, which is a red drink, when Shirley came into the house.

'Are you coming?' said Shirley.

'Yes,' said Ruth. 'Where are we going? I haven't had my breakfast yet.'

'You're on with it, though,' said Shirley. 'Did you spill that drink, or did you put those clothes on this morning?'

'This is all I could find for breakfast,' said Ruth. 'They've taken the cake and the biscuits and the pickled onions, and the cat got the bacon.'

'Which cat?' said Shirley.

'One of ours,' said Ruth. 'We've got ten. Nine thin ones and one fat one.'

'Well, get your blackboard and come on,' said Shirley. 'All the kids are waiting.'

'Oh,' said Ruth. 'School. I was just feeling like lying in the hayfield sucking grass, and then sliding on the pikes.' Pikes are a small sort of haystack, the right size for a tractor to lift and carry away. They are the right size for sliding down if no one is watching them being flattened, and if there is more hay round them to land on.

'You promised to have school in your shippon,' said Shirley. 'Where's the blackboard?'

Ruth finished her drink and brought the board out from behind the clock. 'I'll bring some coloured chalk,' she said. 'I had a box somewhere.' She found the box and picked chalks out of it. 'Blue, green, yellow, brown, two reds, black,' she said, 'I'd better bring two lots of black, too, because it doesn't show up at all on a blackboard, so I have to write it on thick.'

Outside in the sunshine Shirley looked at Ruth. 'You haven't got two colours on the same,' she said. 'Except one sock matches the other.'

'They both do,' said Ruth.

Susan and Bill were waiting for them. Bobby had been in the hayfield, and now he had come back, because there was nothing to do but wait for the sun to dry the grass.

'Fletcher's working,' said Bobby. 'But there's Mary not doing a thing, and Betty and Colin making daisy chains out of buttercups. I'll get them.'

Ruth's shippon was behind the house. On the ground floor the cows were milked, and above was the hay mew, where the hay was kept. Now it was empty, because last year's hay had been used, and this year's was not yet out of the field. The way up to it was by the outside steps and through the red door.

There were no windows. Light came through the door, and between the slates of the roof, and some came up through the floor where the boards gaped. There was a smell of dryness and dust, and a smell of washed floor from the shippon below. A tap dripped on to the concrete.

Ruth stood her blackboard on its edge, and let it drop. It went down with a whoosh and lifted dust and grass seed up all round itself. She had put it down to open the other door of the mew, the forking-hole door, the one that the hay was lifted up through when it was brought.

'They'll be wanting it off when they start leading the hay,' said Ruth. Light flooded in, and sunshine lay on the floor.

Bobby came back with the three he had gone to fetch. There were seven in the mew now, Fletcher in the fields, and eight more unaccounted for.

'We shall have to have your dolls,' said Ruth to Shirley.

'What dolls?' said Shirley.

'Never mind,' said Ruth. 'I'll teach first. Now, all stand behind your desks. Facing me, Bobby. Shirley, show Susan and Bill to their desks. Don't let them fall out of the window.'

Ruth picked up the blackboard and leaned it against the wall. 'We'll have register on the back of it,' she said. 'I'll just write everybody down, and when you've answered your name you can sit down. The ones that aren't here can't sit down.'

The lessons were well on their way when the tractor came to the shippon. Even Bill had learned to say that two and two were four. He thought it was the alphabet. The tractor drove up and stopped outside. Then, without any warning, a bale of hay came in at the forking hole, and rolled into the middle of school. Another one followed it, and hit the first one, and lay blocking the hole.

'Playtime,' said Ruth. She was not going to let bales of hay interrupt lessons. But she had to, because this was the first load of this year's hay, as dry as possible, and smelling fresher than grass itself. Bobby and Shirley hauled the two bales back from the hole, and looked out to say that they were ready for more. It was Ruth's father with the tractor. He was on the load of bales, and was waiting for them to be moved before pitching any more in. He told Ruth to take the nursery out of the mew. Her mother came to move the bales.

'We'll come back in tomorrow,' said Ruth. 'There'll be something to sit on, at least.'

'You can stop out,' said her father. 'I don't want you kids rowking about up there. Off you go.'

'All right,' said Ruth. 'No more school for today. We'll have it in another place tomorrow.'

'And my turn to teach,' said Shirley. 'And I'm going to find a sum book with the answers in the back, then you can't argue.'

The next day they did no better. They began school in the mew behind Shirley's house, but hay began coming in there. They moved to Bobby's father's greenhouse, but they were roasted there, and Bill had his fingers yellowed with the leaves of the tomato plants, and Susan ate five lettuce seedlings. Bobby thought they had better go rather far away and wash Bill's hands. Shirley said the heat had driven her teachings out of her head, and they gave up for the day.

The next day was Friday. The only place they could find for the school was Shirley's garden, so, of course, Shirley had to teach again. That meant she could sit in the swing most of the time. If the pupils gave the right answer they could have a short turn. Instead of having a swing they could have refreshments. The refreshments were glasses of water. Shirley had to get on and off the swing so many times, and fetch so many glasses of water, that she began to ask questions that had no answers, like What was William the Conqueror's middle name? or What is the area of a line five yards long? or Draw and explain a hen. In the end she closed school because Ruth insisted that William the Conqueror's middle name was 'the', and Bobby said the other questions were riddles, and he hadn't learnt anything.

'Do you learn anything at Miss Oldroyd's?' said Shirley.

'No,' said Bobby. 'We just work away. But it's not the same.'

'I'll give you work next time,' said Shirley. 'The trouble is, we've only got one sum book, and I never found the one with the answers in. I wish we'd got more books.'

In the evening Shirley and Ruth were walking back from the hayfield, where they had been secretly sliding down a pike. Ruth's mother was with them. 'No more holiday,' she said. 'You've to go to Burton school on Monday. We had a letter this morning.'

'We would have to go there,' said Shirley. 'Where the pigs fly.'

'My turn to teach on Monday,' said Ruth. 'I know what we'll do. I've been thinking of it all day.'

Chapter Five

VERY late in the evening Fletcher rode back into the village on a load of hay. He had been at work all day, and his arms and face were red from the sun.

He jumped down from the hay wagon and pulled a long stalk of hay from his shirt. Now that he was standing close Ruth could see the layer of dust and pollen that had settled on him, stuck to his sweat.

'That's the last of Low Sike,' he said, naming the field the hay had come from. 'And if the weather stops right we'll have it all by the end of next week.'

'You won't be there,' said Ruth.

'I will that,' said Fletcher. He thought Ruth was talking about his sunburn. His mother had talked about it all day. 'I don't burn, I go brown. I always go red first off, and then I cook through.'

'It's not that,' said Ruth. 'I mean school's starting again.'

'Is she back?' said Fletcher.

'No,' said Ruth. 'They say we have to go to Burton school.'

'I've a cousin there,' said Fletcher. 'But he'll be in the fields the best part of the day.'

'We'll be in school,' said Ruth.

'Pigs flying to market,' said Fletcher. 'We have to learn this and that, maybe.'

Bobby came along to see how his friend was doing. Bobby did not like working in the fields, and if he could get out of it he did, and if he couldn't get out of it he did as little as possible.

'Hello,' said Fletcher. 'Here's Hercules. What have you been on with, Bobby?'

'Laiking on,' said Bobby. He had been playing all day.

'We've been leading hay,' said Fletcher. 'This is the last lot tonight.' His father had opened the gate and was driving the tractor through into the yard. Fletcher climbed back on to the load and travelled the last few yards to the mew. Bobby thought he would stop being lazy for the time being, and went after Fletcher up into the mew, to clear the hay back from the forking hole as it came in.

Ruth went home. She had already gone up to bed, but the long light night had brought her out again, really to see Shirley. Shirley, though, was behind curtains and on her way to sleep. Ruth went home and through the dairy window, because the doors were locked. She was last up.

The next day was Saturday. The white sun was searching the walls before Ruth was up. She watched it hanging like a window in the trees. It was too bright to look at when it came higher. Even early in the morning the paint on the window was distilling its turpentine and softening into blisters.

Milk cans banged on the milk stand. Cutter bars were chewing their way across fields again, and when the dew had lifted the tedders were dashing the hay into the air and releasing the summery smell of the drying grass.

Ruth had to go into the field. There was no time for sliding down pikes or for making hay houses. She had to use a rake all the morning, windrowing the steep hill side, ready for the tractor to pick up the long hay hills she had made. The hay had to be taken down on to the flat part of the field to be put up into pikes and wait for the baler, which came round in turn when it could.

When it came it had to be fed. It did not come in the afternoon, though it was expected. It did not come at tea time, nor at seven. In the end it came near nine o'clock, when it was about to be given up. The pikes were broken down again, and the hay went in loose. The sun set, and the baler laid its newly wrapped bales one at a time on the ground. Ruth and her mother pulled them aside as they came and stood them on end. Twilight came, and the place where they worked became more and more shadowy, with the baler at one side and the bales standing like stone circles at the other.

In the end the owner of the baler switched off the engine, and there was a sudden silence that seemed to come from far away. 'That's all for now,' said the owner of the baler. 'We can't see tonight. We'll start again in the morning.'

'Monday morning,' said Ruth's father, because the next day was Sunday. Ruth sat on a bale, and looked out into the night. The owner of the baler looked at his watch by the light of a match. 'Gone eleven,' he

said. 'No wonder we can't see. Another half hour and it'd be Sunday.'

They went back through the dark village. Ruth thought she was last up again, until she saw Fletcher carrying a lantern across his yard. He looked quite black tonight, but Ruth thought that was more to do with the lantern light than with the sunlight.

Morning had well gone when Shirley woke her up. Shirley had been up a long time, had breakfast, played by herself for more than an hour, and then come looking for Ruth.

'Tell mum to get my breakfast ready for me,' said Ruth. 'I haven't woken up before. I've slept too long,

Shirley. I'll get a headache and be in a bad temper. I warn you.'

'You'll be in a worse one tomorrow when you have to get up and go to school,' said Shirley. 'If you aren't, I will be.'

'I don't mind school,' said Ruth. 'Go and tell my mum about breakfast. I want a bacon sandwich with the bacon so that it breaks, and coffee, and chocolate biscuits, and then I want all my clothes so that I can get up.'

Shirley went to see what she could get, and came back with clothes only, because Ruth had to go down for breakfast.

'It's a hard life,' said Ruth. 'The last day of our holiday, too. They ought to be extra kind. They don't know what it's like to be young and dreadful.'

Shirley put the clothes the right way out, and shook them so that hay flew all over the room. Ruth dressed, turned the bathroom taps on and off quickly, dried the tips of her fingers, which were the only things that had got wet, and went down.

Shirley was wondering how they would go to Burton school. Ruth thought they would walk over the fields, because there was no bus through the village except on Fridays, and Sunday afternoons. When the bus did come it would not take you to Burton.

'It'll rain,' said Shirley. 'And we'll have to walk all the way back.'

'Actually,' said Ruth. 'I've had a good idea.'

'Yes,' said Shirley. 'What is it?' She was not going to guess at anything, because Ruth's idea might be about anything she was doing at the time, not about the thing you expected, the thing you were talking about.

'Putting butter and marmalade on the top of the sandwich,' said Ruth. 'Then you eat breakfast in one.'

'I thought it would be something like that,' said Shirley. But she was sure that Ruth had been going to say something else quite different, and had changed her mind at the last minute.

'It wasn't that, was it?' she said.

'It must have been,' said Ruth. 'Or I wouldn't have been able to say it, would I? I can't say things I haven't thought of, can I?'

'Yes,' said Shirley. She thought, Ruth could.

'We'll all go together,' said Ruth.

'Where'll we go?' said Shirley. 'And who?'

'Us. To school,' said Ruth. 'We don't want people all straggling in the fields. You know Fletcher, he'd be off making hay and all that. And Bill and Susan would get lost. It's their first day.'

'Oh,' said Shirley, 'they aren't coming until Miss Oldroyd gets back. I saw them. Susan was crying, but it might have been about something else; and Bill wants to learn the next alphabet, so they might come with us.'

'They've got to,' said Ruth. 'That's what school's for. We can't have it without them.'

Chapter Six

BILL'S mother, and Susan's mother, wondered whether it would really be all right to send their children to school when they had been invited to stay away.

'We'll look after them,' said Ruth. 'Shirley and me. No one else could.'

'But if the teacher doesn't want them,' said Bill's mother.

'Oh, she does,' said Ruth. 'And we'll see they don't get lost on the way or fall in the beck or leave their shoes behind or don't take a towel. And they don't use ink at that age, so you haven't got that to worry about.'

'I wasn't worrying about that,' said Bill's mother. 'But it's a long walk, and a long day; and I don't really want him to go even when he has to. Poor little Bill.' Then she changed her mind again. 'If you'll keep an eye on him,' she said. 'I know he wants to be off, and I can't do anything about that.'

Ruth and Shirley walked back to the middle of the village and started to play catchings on the green. Bobby came out to help and tease a bit, so Ruth changed the game to Block, and when Bobby had hidden himself she and Shirley went home to tea.

'He'll still be there in the morning,' said Shirley. 'We don't mind, do we?'

'We want him then,' said Ruth. 'Not before.'

Bobby had gone home long before that, of course. He came out of his house in the morning and waited in the road to see who he would go to school with. Fletcher came along the street, sprouting with the hay that had stuck into his clothes. Against the light he looked almost furry. He was grumbling about having to go to school. He would rather be in the fields.

'They'd rather have me there, too,' he said.

'Who would? Miss Oldroyd?' said Bobby. Fletcher picked up a stone and threw it at a row of birds on a wire. The birds whirred their wings like clockwork and flew to another wire.

Ruth was waiting indoors. She did not want to be out first, or last, or at the wrong moment in the middle. She waited until she felt it was the right time to go into the road; just as Shirley came out of her door.

'Shall I get Bill and Susan?' said Shirley.

'Yes,' said Ruth. 'You do that. I'll keep all the others together.'

Shirley looked at Ruth with care. 'Are you a sheep-dog?' she said. 'Or just bossy?'

'It must be the thing I thought of,' said Ruth. 'I don't want to be bossy. I just thought we could all walk together like a school.'

'We can walk with ourselves,' said Bobby. 'Can't you, Fletcher?'

'I can,' said Fletcher. 'I will, and all.'

'No, wait,' said Ruth. Fletcher waited, because he did not want to start for school before he must.

43

Shirley walked along with Bill and Susan, one on either side. The rest of the children came up one by one. There were sixteen altogether: Ruth, Shirley, Bobby, Mary, Fletcher, Peter, Ann, Jenny, Betty, Colin, George, Ann, Janet, David, Susan, and Bill. Everybody was present.

'Let's go,' said Ruth. 'We've got plenty of time, and I know the best way.'

'You've thought of something,' said Shirley. 'I think you've thought of something, Ruth.'

'I know,' said Ruth. 'Come on.'

The way to Burton was down the road, starting off the way they always went to school. Usually Miss Oldroyd's little car would overtake them as they walked, and sometimes she would give a lift to a little one on a wet day. It used to be Janet and David who were littlest, but now it was Susan and Bill. But there was no Miss Oldroyd, and it was a fine day.

Down the hill and round the corner was the stile that led the path through the fields. Ruth got to it first and stood in it. 'Well,' she said, 'we can't go this way. I've just remembered. There's a bull in one of the fields.'

'There never is,' said Fletcher. 'Whose bull? Which field?'

'I've got a feeling about it,' said Ruth. 'We'll have to go round by the road and through the fields the other side. It isn't any further, because Burton school's right at the top of the village.'

'And then the shop's the wrong side of it,' said Bobby. 'We'd have gone past it this way.'

'And past the bull,' said Shirley. She did not believe

44

in the bull, but she did believe in Ruth. Ruth had something in mind. Ruth would not say what it was.

They came to the bottom of the hill and crossed the bridge. Here they should have turned left and gone up the road a little way, but Ruth said they were to go to the right.

'Why?' said Fletcher. 'We're getting further from Burton now, not going nearer at all.'

'The stile's blocked up,' said Shirley, because Ruth was hesitating a bit about what to say.

'They haven't cut that field yet,' said Ruth. 'We don't want to be tramping in it and laying it.'

'You're both wrong,' said Fletcher. 'But we'll do what you want.'

Ruth smiled a knowing smile. 'We'll get there,' she said. She led them to the right. 'There's another stile up here,' she said.

'We're nearly at the old school,' said Bobby. 'Where we did go once.'

'Oh, aye,' said Ruth. 'There's its roof.'

'Miles off Burton,' said Fletcher. 'You couldn't start from home and get further away, I shouldn't think. Not and still be so near.'

'That road's much twistier than you think,' said Ruth. 'It goes miles and miles round, so you're always miles and miles off Burton, and when you've got to Burton you're still miles and miles off Burton school.'

'And the shop,' said Bobby.

'Come on,' said Ruth. 'Susan and Bill aren't grumbling.'

The others walked behind Ruth, looking for the stile she had promised them. They did not find one on

the left side of the road, where they thought it ought to be.

'There isn't one,' said Fletcher. 'I can't think of it.'

'Nor can I,' said Bobby.

'There it is,' said Shirley. But it was the wrong side of the road, on the right, and no one knew where it led. It certainly would never take them to Burton.

'I'm off back,' said Bobby. 'We'll be late.'

'No,' said Ruth. 'We can't be late. I know we won't be.'

'It's daft,' said Bobby. 'We're going right past our own school. Look, there it is in the road, and everybody knows it isn't on the way to Burton. It's on a road that never goes near.'

'We aren't going past our own school,' said Ruth. 'The trouble with you is you don't even know where you're going. Anyway, you can give up quarrelling with me, because I won't have it.'

Bobby said he wasn't bothered where he got to, and it wasn't his fault. Shirley told Ruth that Miss Oldroyd was the one who wouldn't have things, generally.

'It's me today,' said Ruth. 'It's my turn, you know.'

They came to their own school. The road stretched on beyond it.

'I told you,' said Bobby. 'We'll have to go past it.'

'Oh,' said Shirley. 'Of course.'

'Of course,' said Ruth. But she and Shirley meant something different from what Bobby meant.

'We won't go past,' said Ruth. 'We'll go in.'

She put her hand in the hole in the wall and brought out the key. She put it in the lock, turned it, lifted the latch, and pushed the door open.

Out came the smell of school, of desks and paper and ink and pencil-sharpening, of paint and flowers and glue, of chalk and books and chairs.

'Come on,' she said. 'Time for lessons to begin.'

Chapter Seven

'Nay, lass,' said Fletcher. 'You don't know which end of the week it is. Where do you think you're at?'

'School,' said Ruth. 'You know the place.'

'I knew the spot,' said Fletcher.

'Then come in,' said Ruth. She stepped inside herself, and her footsteps echoed back from the walls and the roof.

'It's easy,' said Shirley. 'Just walk in.' She followed Ruth, and stood with her in the middle of the big classroom floor. Fletcher and Bobby stood in the doorway and looked in. The others looked over their shoulders and between them; but no one came in.

Then someone began to push his way through among the legs. His head came into the class room, and then his shoulders, turned sideways to get through the narrow gap between Bobby and Fletcher. It was Bill. His face was red with pushing. He did not know it would be such a hard job to get into school. After him came Susan. It was easier for her, because Bill had cleared the way. Bill stood up, and put back a hand for Susan. He looked round, sniffed the air, and said: 'Where do we have to sit, Ruth?'

'Oh, I don't know yet,' said Ruth. 'We'll have to get another desk for you. We'll get all the others sitting down first. It isn't quite school time yet. There's another ten minutes.'

'Time to get to Burton,' said Fletcher. 'I'll win you, Bobby. This lot can stop where it likes.'

Ruth left the middle of the room. She came to the doorway, took Fletcher by the shoulder, kicked him on the ankle, and dragged him on one foot to his desk and pushed him into it. He sat there and rubbed his ankle.

'This is your school, and don't you forget it,' said Ruth.

Shirley thought she should treat Bobby the same way, but he was ready for her. It was Shirley who sat in the desk and Bobby who stood in the middle of the room.

'Thank you, Bobby,' said Ruth, in her best Miss Oldroyd manner. 'I was just waiting for someone to be sensible enough to help me. Now all you others come in and we'll start.'

'Too early,' said Fletcher. 'You've nearly fetched blood out of my ankle.'

'I couldn't do, with sandals,' said Ruth. 'Let's hear no more of you.'

The rest of the school came in and sat down. Ruth opened the cupboard where Miss Oldroyd kept the books, and brought out the Register.

'Quiet whilst I fill it,' she said. 'Shirley, please will you alter the calendar. It always says the wrong day and the wrong date.'

Shirley got up from her desk and turned the calendar to the right day. She was not sure of the date, but the day was more important.

'Thank you,' said Ruth. 'Now I'm going to start another page, and if anyone doesn't behave I shall put their names on it, ready for Miss Oldroyd. She'll know what to do with anyone who's naughty.'

'I won't be naughty,' said Fletcher. 'I'll be right wicked when I think of it.'

'I'll put you down each time,' said Ruth. 'Now we'll get the dinner money.' She put away the register and brought out the dinner book and the cash box where the dinner money went. Shirley took the box round and counted up the sixteen people, and told Ruth how many there were.

'Thank you,' said Ruth. 'Now we'll have prayers, when I've put the books away.'

She put the books back in the cupboard, and the cash box on top of them, and closed the cupboard. Miss Oldroyd always went to the piano now, and played a hymn. Ruth went to the piano, and looked at it. She had hoped that she would suddenly know how to play a hymn, because so far she had been as good as Miss Oldroyd at her job. But the piano just looked at her with its black and white teeth, without any helpful expression on its face at all.

'Well,' said Ruth, 'we know the hymns. We'll have "There is a Green Hill", and we'll just have to sing it loudly together.'

Whilst the hymn was being sung Ruth found the little book of school prayers, and chose one from it, and they had that. Then she told them they could all open their eyes.

51

'Now it's my turn,' said Shirley. 'You've done all the best parts. I'll teach for a bit.'

'No,' said Ruth. 'You were teacher the last time we had a school. You can't be teacher again. It's your turn tomorrow. You can be the top child and do all the things like cleaning the board and making holes in the milk tops and getting out the paints and the plasticine.'

'And I'll teach tomorrow,' said Shirley. 'And then and then.' She meant that after that they would take it in turn and turn about, day by day.

'And then and then,' said Ruth, turning her hands round each other just as Shirley had done. 'And you needn't start doing it, Fletcher. We'll start with arithmetic.' She got out Miss Oldroyd's book and opened it.

It was the book with answers in. 'It's page seventeen,' she said. 'And page six.' She meant that the big ones were to do the hard sums, and the middle ones the easier ones. There was something else for the very little ones, and she would have to be teaching them whilst the others did the sums.

'Just begin at the beginning of the page,' said Shirley, because she knew she was looking after the top part of the school.

'I'll tell you the answers later,' said Ruth. 'I can't do the sums as well as teach the little ones adding.'

She took the little ones into a corner and taught them to write their figures. First of all, though, she sharpened their pencils for them in the sharpener, whether they needed it or not. Then she gave Bill and Susan a new book each from the cupboard, put their names on the covers, and made them a neat row of numbers to copy. Then she had to hold Bill's hand whilst he made 5's, because it kept facing the wrong way for him. Susan did not quite understand about making figures like the ones at the top of the page, and she had to have her hand held in turn. The others had all done figures before, but still George liked to make his 3's lying down flat on their faces.

Shirley finished her page of sums, and came up to the desk to ask whether they were right.

'I haven't done them myself,' said Ruth. 'You look after the little ones, and I'll do them before looking at the answers.'

When the sums were done and marked they had history. Ruth thought it would be the easiest thing to do, because she only had to read out from the book and ask questions, and if there was any time over they could all draw.

By the time she had read, and asked the questions, and they had all made their drawings, it was half past ten.

'Put your books away,' said Ruth. 'Playtime. Shirley's going to see to the milk.'

'The beakers are all dusty,' said Shirley. 'I saw when I came in. I'll have to rinse them all first, before I pour the milk in.'

She went through to the cloakroom and rinsed the beakers under the tap, and put them on the tray. She came back into the schoolroom with the tray and put it on the table. They heard her rattle the wire crate the milk came in, and she came in again.

'There isn't any milk,' she said. 'They haven't brought it. It hasn't come.'

'Good,' said Ruth. 'We needn't have any. I hate milk.'

'What a waste of washing,' said Shirley. 'But they'll do for tomorrow.'

They had playtime without milk, and then more lessons, until twelve o'clock, when they brought out the tables and laid them for dinner. Half-way through the laying Shirley stopped. She put away the forks she was holding. 'You know,' she said. 'There isn't any dinner either. No one came and cooked it. No one knows we're here.'

'They must have,' said Ruth. 'It's their job.' She went through to the kitchen, and saw the stove cold in its corner, the table empty, the pans hung on their hooks. No one had been there to make the dinner. Even the water in the tap was cold.

'I never thought of it,' she said. 'But we'll eat the sweets in the tin instead. We'll have two each.'

'Grand meal,' said Fletcher. 'Is it like this all the week?'

'Of course not,' said Ruth. She hoped it wouldn't be, she meant, but she did not know quite what to do. 'Today we'll only stay half the time we should, but we'll have dinner tomorrow if I have to cook it myself.'

'You hope,' said Fletcher.

'We all do,' said Bobby.

Chapter Eight

THEY all went home very soon. It was one thing to have lessons in a make-believe sort of way, but it was another to have dinner only in your imagination. There was very nearly a strike of pupils. Bobby ate well down his pencil, and Fletcher made deep tooth-marks across the corner of his English book. His teeth were not sharp enough to bite right through the corner, but his spit was wet enough to make the ink on the cover run and give him a bluish beard.

'It's the way my mouth waters,' he said.

'All right,' said Ruth. 'Hands together, close your eyes. We'll say our prayer and go home.'

Ruth and Shirley were left to walk home alone, because they had stayed behind to tidy up. Someone had to do it. Shirley picked a ripe stem of grass and chewed it.

'I'm famished,' she said. 'What shall we do? You'll have to do it yourself whilst I'm teaching.'

'Mary Croft generally comes to cook,' said Ruth. 'Why didn't she today? Perhaps she doesn't come when there isn't any school. They didn't expect us. Shall we tell her we're there, and then she would come? I thought things just went on happening, like dinners being cooked every day except Saturday and Sunday.'

'Who would eat them?' said Shirley.

'Not us,' said Ruth. 'They *weren't* cooked, after all.'

'What are we going to have, then?' said Shirley. 'You'll have to buy the things tonight, won't you?'

Ruth saw that that was the only thing to do. They went back to the school and brought out the box of dinner money. 'It's what it's for,' said Shirley. 'It isn't stealing or anything.'

'Nothing like that,' said Ruth. 'Isn't there a lot here?'

'Sixteen people at five shillings,' said Shirley. 'I'll just work it out on the board. It's four pounds. Four whole pounds.'

There was more than four pounds in the box, because some money was always left in it for giving change. Ruth sorted out four pounds and left the rest in the box. Then she counted the rest of the days in the week, which were Tuesday to Friday, inclusive, and were four. 'It's a pound a day,' she said. 'Have I got to spend a whole pound on shopping? It's much too much. It couldn't cost a pound a day.'

'I'll do the sum,' said Shirley. 'It should have done for five days, not four. Eighty, that's shillings, and five into it, one and three over and into thirty five ones are five twos are ten threes are fifteen fours twenty-five one more thirty goes exactly none over sixteen multiply remainder by twelve makes nothing again. It's sixteen shillings a day.'

'That's not enough,' said Ruth. 'Only a shilling each. But if it's a pound that's only one and three each, but it seems a lot more.'

'We'll have big helpings,' said Shirley. 'Bring a whole pound.'

They took a ten shilling note, and five florins, wrapped them up firmly in each other, and put the cash box away. Shirley cleaned the sum off the board and clapped her chalky hands. They went home.

After tea they made a list, not of things, but of people in school, and took it to the shop, with a basket, and bought what they thought would be exactly enough: three potatoes each, or two large ones, for the top class, two potatoes each, or one big one, for the middle class, and one each for the little ones. They bought three tins of meat, the soft sweet sort. Ruth thought that if she cut the meat in even slices that the slices from the top of the tin would be smaller than the slices from the other end, and that different ends of the tin would do for different ends of the school, because the tins tapered. They bought forty-eight plums, which was three each, and then they were within a penny of being able to buy a big tin of condensed milk. They were so near it that they were allowed it at a penny less than the usual price.

The next morning they put all the stores in Ruth's dolls' pram, which she still had, because of not wanting to give up dolls. Shirley would not push it, because she wanted to give up playing with them, but still loved them dreadfully. Ruth pushed it, with Susan helping.

'I would be ashamed to help you if it had a doll in it,' said Shirley, 'and I would feel cruel to push it when it only has potatoes in. It makes the potatoes seem alive, and then we've got to eat them.'

Ruth went straight into the school kitchen when

they got there. The kitchen staff did not join in prayers and lessons. She arranged the kitchen to her liking by moving the table against the wall and opening the window, and settled down to making the dinner.

She switched on the water heater, being rather careful about moving the switch, in case it sparked or boiled over or did anything she could not understand. She opened the store cupboard, and found the sugar and salt and tea for playtime, the kettle and the tea pot.

She washed the plums and put them into a big pan with some water. When she had done it the pan was too heavy to be put on the stove first. She put in a good lot of sugar, nearly all there was.

In the schoolroom she could hear Shirley keeping order and teaching Bill and Susan the middle of the alphabet at the same time. Ruth tipped all the potatoes into the sink and started on the first one. A wasp came in and looked at the plums, then went out again. Ruth put the lid on the pan and turned on the stove. She went back to her potatoes. Usually they were done in the machine, which was somehow joined to the tap, but she had no idea how it worked. She had to cut off the skin by hand and winkle out the eyes, and rinse and rinse the mud away. Her hands began to be washerwoman's hands, and the potato peel began to stick to her wrists.

At half past ten she put on the kettle and made a pot of tea. There was no milk to have with it. She took the pot through for Shirley, who did not mind about the milk. Instead she put in more sugar. There was only a very little left in the bottom of the packet now. Ruth went back into the kitchen and wrote 'Sugar' on the slate.

The plums boiled over. Two wasps came to look and have a steam bath. Ruth prodded the plums with a fork, and left them to cook a little longer. They were very sweet, she found, when she licked the fork.

In a little while she had to close the kitchen window to keep out the wasps. She put out sixteen helpings of plums, measuring each plateful fairly, and then put the potatoes to cook. She opened the condensed milk and let it drain into the jug, and then stood a moment and let the last drops drain into her mouth, before throwing the tin into the bucket. She lifted the little keys of the tinned meat and opened the tins. The meat had to be persuaded out of the tin with a fork. Then she cut it up very exactly, and made different sized platefuls for the different classes. There was a slice left

over. She looked at it several times, and then cut it in four, and four fours again, and shared it out. She licked her fingers.

Dinner was ready on time. The potatoes were drained and dry and shared out by the time the tables were up. The plums were given their dressing of yellow milk, spoon by spoon, and the spoon licked. The pans were in to soak, and everything was exactly right.

'That's better,' said Fletcher. 'But there isn't plenty of potatoes, that's all.'

'All this meal cost a pound,' said Ruth. 'A whole pound. And a penny, which we got given.'

They shared the washing up after the meal, swept the kitchen, and began lessons again, with art. Today it was plasticine patterns on paper, which smells nice and doesn't make too much mess unless it is trodden into the floor. They were in the middle of it when there was a chirrup from the corner of the room, startling everybody. It was the telephone. It rang, buzz-buzz, buzz-buzz, and no one dared go near it. Then it stopped, and there was silence. 'Let's go home,' said Shirley. 'We've been in here long enough today.'

Chapter Nine

THE next morning there was a trickle of water coming out from under the school door, when they came to it. Ruth had a feeling that the whole school was full of water, and that when the door was opened it would rush out and sweep them all away, and the desks and the blackboard and the piano, even the telephone, would ride out on the wave.

'Open it very sweetly,' said Shirley.

'Hm,' said Ruth. 'A pipe must have burst.'

She put the key in the lock and turned it. She twisted the handle of the door, and pushed. She opened it half an inch. There was only air behind it. The water was on the floor and not half-way up the walls. She could hear it running on to the floor somewhere.

She opened the door wide and went in. The running water was in the cloakroom. The afternoon before they had come out of school in such a hurry that the person getting a drink of clean water from the filter had not had time to turn it off. It had been running slowly all night, into the sink. There was a towel in the sink, and the towel had blocked the drain, and the water was trickling over the edge, across the floor, and out into the road. Ruth held her skirt, because she was

going wading, and walked across to the filter. She turned it off, leaned over and pulled the towel out of the plug hole. The water in the sink drained away, gurgled in the throat of the pipe, said 'Blop', and lay winking down below the brass grating, like an eye.

Ruth waded back across the wet floor.

'You look very funny doing that,' said Shirley. 'The water isn't deep enough to measure, but you look as if you feel it was around your knees.'

'I was feeling very brave,' said Ruth. 'It was a waste of feeling, though. We shouldn't have gone out in such a hurry, yesterday. The teacher should have stayed behind and made sure everything was all right.'

'I wouldn't dare,' said Shirley. 'Not with that thing ringing. But it's stopped now.'

Shirley was to do the cooking today. So far they had not even bought the food for dinner, because they had left all the dinner money behind, coming out in such a hurry. They had left the pram as well. Shirley was to go back to the village and buy what she needed, whilst Ruth went on with the lessons. She would not take the pram, though, in case anyone saw her with such a thing. She thought Betty could wheel the pram for her, with one of the school puppets in it, under a duster, to make her look like a little girl taking a doll for a ride, instead of a school caterer's assistant fetching the groceries.

'Whilst you're gone we'll clean up,' said Ruth. 'It'll use up a lesson, and we can't wipe the wet off our feet because the doormat's as wet as a fish itself.'

Shirley hopped into the schoolroom, took off her

shoes, and took a pound out of the cash box. Ruth reminded her to look on the slate in the kitchen, and to take the list of pupils that had to be given dinner, so that she could buy the right amount of each thing, and something different for those that didn't like what she was giving the rest.

When Shirley had gone, with Betty arranging the puppet to look comfortable, Ruth picked up the wet doormat and threw it into the road. It lay there sad and curled, with water running from its corners. Then she set the rest of the school on to moving everything out of the cloakroom, through the front door, and round into the yard, with Mary and Ann to dry and dust everything as it came. They even emptied the long cupboard, which was full of mouldering books, orphan gym shoes, skipping ropes, dead footballs, a globe of the world, a globe of the sky, the watering can, a whole box of green chalk, seven hair-slides, a tea-spoon with a very neat hole drilled through it, four rolls of blue paper for drawing, and a large spider that did not agree with spring cleaning. Fletcher picked it up and carried it out of the building and let it go on the far side of the road. He said it was so big he could feel its weight.

They mopped the floor dry, opened the windows, came out through the front door, and into school through the yard and the kitchen. Ruth locked the front door, so that no one would start running through until the floor was dry. Then she dragged the door mat into the yard, and shook it, which made no difference to it, and laid it in the sun. That made very little difference too.

Ruth was in a cleaning mood now. Everybody except Shirley and Betty was in school. She thought she had better not mark the register yet, or there would be two missing, and without the register school could not begin. She thought they could tidy the schoolroom. The pupils all agreed with her, because it was different from lessons.

They emptied the window ledges, and helped the boys up to clean the glass. They made little mountains in the middle of the room, so that the boys, when they had finished the windows, could go and dust the lampshades. They moved the piano and swept under it, and took the board down off the wall and washed it, and left it in the sun to dry streaky. They emptied all the cupboards in the room, and put a duster across the shelves inside. They took down all the pictures on the wall and put them up again in another order. Ruth very bravely went to the telephone and dusted that. They watered the flowers. They threw away a stump of chalk and put out a longer piece. It was a piece of the green out of the box in the cloakroom cupboard.

Bobby saw Shirley and Betty coming down the hill, from where he was breathing on the window and shining it.

'Quick,' said Ruth. 'Come and dust the lamps, and put everything back and pretend we've been doing work.'

'We have been,' said Bobby. 'But not scholar's work.'

They had everything almost back by the time Shirley came in, humping the pram over the threshold into the kitchen. Betty came through with the puppet and the duster, and Shirley came through with fourpence change.

'I nearly bought sweets with it,' she said. 'But I didn't think it was real food, so I didn't.'

'We wouldn't have minded,' said Ruth. 'The tin's a bit low. We've just been tidying up. We wanted to finish before you came back, but we didn't quite. I was just going to do that cupboard up there by the door.'

'I've never seen inside it,' said Shirley. 'You might as well do it now, and then we can have a look.'

The cupboard was locked. The door did not even have a handle. It would need a key, to unlock it, and the key would have to do for a handle too. Ruth rattled the door, but locked it was. She ran the duster over the top, and that was all she could do to it.

'I wonder what it is,' said Shirley. 'It wouldn't be treasure. They don't have it in these days. Perhaps she keeps all the answers up there. You never know.'

By now it was playtime. Shirley put on the kettle and made herself and the teacher a cup of tea, before settling down to peeling the potatoes. 'I got some sugar,' she said, and opened the packet. Ruth took the packet, and because there was no milk being brought to school, she took it round to each person in turn, for them to lick a finger and dip it in the white grains, for something to suck on until dinner was ready.

At the end of playtime they listened to the schools' programme on the wireless for a whole hour. Dinner should have been ready by then, but the potatoes wanted another ten minutes' cooking and five minutes' serving. They listened to the next programme until the dinner was on the plates.

After dinner Ruth thought they should really have lessons, of the arithmetic sort. She thought they had to teach Bill and Susan to read and write before Miss Oldroyd came back; and perhaps she might be able to teach Fletcher about fractions as well. He did not really understand what the line between the two figures did.

They were half through the lesson when someone came to the door. Whoever it was did not knock, but lifted the latch. The door was still locked, to keep people off the wet floor. The visitor shook the door a second time, and then seemed to go away. Bobby looked out of the window to see who it was.

'It's a man in a cap, one of those blue caps with a edge,' he said. 'I think he's an inspector. They have them for schools, like on buses.'

Chapter Ten

'INSPECTOR,' said Shirley. 'I've done the washing up, anyway.'

'He inspects us,' said Ruth. 'And the teachers. That's me. He might ask me questions, and I don't know them. What shall we do?'

'Nowt,' said Bobby. 'That fellow's off. He's got in his car and gone away.'

'He'll come back,' said Ruth. 'Everybody has to be very good. Bill and Susan have got to learn everything straight away. Fletcher, you've got to know fractions.'

'I'll learn the thirteen times table,' said Shirley.

'There isn't one,' said Bobby. 'If there is, you can keep it to yourself, whatever.'

No one else came to the door. Towards the end of school-time Ruth turned the key again, and they brought back all the things they had taken out, and put them in their places again. After that they had prayers and went home.

In the morning there was a white square on the mat inside the door. Ruth picked it up and turned it over. It was a postcard addressed to The Principal.

'It means Head Teacher,' said Ruth. 'That's you, Shirley. You'd better read it.'

'I'm a Princessipal, really,' said Shirley, taking the card. 'Perhaps we just ought to put it on her desk and let it wait for her.'

'It's not like a letter,' said Ruth. 'It might be from her to us, mightn't it? What if we hadn't read it.'

In a moment, though, it had been read, or at least looked at. It was headed VENDALE PRIMARY INTERSCHOOLS SPORTS, and went on to say that the sports would be held in a fortnight's time, and that entries should be in in a week's time. Then there was a list of the events, to remind the teachers in case they had forgotten.

'We can't go to that,' said Shirley. 'We don't even know where to send the answer to, or where the sports are, or anything.'

'We'll rowk in the cupboard and find out,' said Ruth.

Before school began they searched in the cupboard where Miss Oldroyd kept everything, and found the folder with SPORTS written on it. It had in it another list of events, with a name and address at the bottom to reply to, and a postcard already written, and addressed, and even stamped. The postcard only had to have some numbers written on it, and be signed, and the school's name and address put on it, and the entry would be made.

'We can send it off,' said Ruth. 'How many shall we put down?'

'It says Competitors and Spectators,' said Shirley. 'Shall I put sixteen of each?'

'Eight of each,' said Ruth. 'At least, I don't know,

because sometimes people will be running or jumping and sometimes they'll be watching.'

They looked at the rules again, and found that each school was supposed to find two people who were best at each event, and put them in as competitors, and the rest could watch.

'We did it last year,' said Shirley. 'I think the competitors are everybody, and the spectators are parents and little sisters.'

'And dogs,' said Ruth.

When they had remembered about doing it before they knew what to do. They had to find the two people best at each event.

'Oh heck,' said Ruth, 'and I'm no good at sports. I'm glad I'm cooking the dinner.'

'I'm just as bad,' said Shirley. 'I would cook the dinner if you would teach.'

'We'll both cook the dinner,' said Ruth. 'And Bobby and Fletcher can teach. They like it.'

Bobby and Fletcher thought that was a very good idea. They would never have agreed to being taught sports by the girls, in any case. 'I don't know about fractions,' said Fletcher. 'But I can high jump and long jump and relay and run.'

They practised in the field behind the school. 'Where I can keep an eye on them,' said Shirley, opening the kitchen window over the field.

Bobby and Fletcher carried out the two stands that held the rail for the high jump, and the pegs that held the tape for the long jump. They took the tape measure that wound back into itself when its middle was pressed; and a pencil and the list of events.

'There, isn't it lovely,' said Shirley. 'All the kids out there in the sun, and us in the kitchen getting the dinner ready, and not even boring old beds to make.'

With two of them at the potatoes the work seemed to be more than twice as easy, even though one of them was always watching the rest outside, to see that they weren't just playing. 'It's all part of school,' said Ruth. 'They're learning, aren't they?'

'They're very good,' said Shirley. 'Can't we give them a treat? Isn't there anything in the cupboard?'

There was a lot of kitchen stuff in the cupboard, things like baking powder and cream of tartar and powdered ginger and cloves and greaseproof paper and suet.

'Some of these things ought to be used up,' said Ruth. 'What can you do with suet?'

'Make a bag pudding,' said Shirley. 'But I don't know how.'

At the back of the shelf was something useful: a bottle of squash. They were able to give the breathless sportsmen and sportswomen a treat by taking them a tray of beakers and two jugs of squash.

'Better than milk,' said Fletcher. 'For just getting the sweat off your tongue. But you can't live on it.'

After dinner, when the list was full, and they knew that eleven people were the best at sports, three were worst, and two had not even tried, because they were cooking the dinner, Shirley tried to begin lessons again.

'We've given that up,' said Fletcher. 'We've been on at it for days. We want a bit of a rest.'

'You didn't do anything all morning,' said Shirley. 'Just sit down and take out your book, and we'll do

English, reading all round the class, and the little ones can draw drawings.'

Susan, the littlest one, licked her crayon. Bill said he wanted to run about a bit more.

'That's right,' said Bobby. 'We have to practise, you know.'

'No you don't,' said Shirley. Bobby was moving towards the door, but Shirley got there first, and locked it against him. Then she stood against the other door. Bobby went to the blackboard and made the chalk squeak on it. Ruth tidied her hair with her hand, stood up at her desk, and began to read from the reading book.

'Very good, Ruth,' said Shirley. 'Not quite so fast, dear.' She said it in a Miss Oldroyd voice, and Ruth's mouth began to shake round the words she was making, because she wanted to laugh at Shirley being Miss Oldroyd.

'Whilst Ruth's reading I'll just mark down the names of the bad people on the list for Miss Oldroyd,' said Shirley. 'Bill, Fletcher, Bobby, Peter . . .'

Bill sat down and got out his crayons and started to draw at double rate. Fletcher took out his reading book. Bobby put the chalk down on the ledge and rubbed off the squeak marks. Peter had only been watching, but now he sat up and listened to Ruth.

'Good,' said Shirley. 'The best person can post this card for me when school is over.'

'Please will you lift me up to the box,' said Bill.

'If you're best,' said Shirley. 'And if everybody's best, we'll have more practices tomorrow.'

In the end Bill was best, because Fletcher dropped his desk lid, Bobby put his finger in the ink, Peter made a Chinese face at Mary, and the others hadn't been naughty, so there was nothing for them to be gooder than. Bill carried the card up to the village, and Susan had to be given a ride in the pram, amongst all the dust from the potatoes.

Chapter Eleven

'You've taught three times this week,' said Shirley.

'I will have, by the end of the day,' said Ruth. 'And you will next week.'

'And it was sports all yesterday morning,' said Shirley. 'So I didn't have a proper go. And now, you see, I'm getting a bit bored of it, even when I haven't managed to do any.'

'It doesn't matter what you feel today,' said Ruth. 'I'm teacher.'

Shirley was a little offended, because Ruth did not give her enough sympathy, or even offer her an extra turn. When Fletcher and Bobby began to be rebellious before they got into school Shirley watched, instead of doing something useful like pulling Fletcher's hair. Ruth had to threaten them with being sent to Burton school, as well as with the list to show Miss Oldroyd, before they would come into the school building. Then she had to pinch the backs of their necks to make them sit down. They sat down and rubbed their necks. Shirley went into the kitchen.

'Register,' said Ruth. 'That'll show if you're here, Fletcher, and if you aren't we'll get the kidcatcher and you'll get put in the dogs' home;' and she looked fiercely at Fletcher.

Shirley spoiled Ruth's bad temper by giggling behind the kitchen door.

'Well,' said Ruth, 'somebody has to catch the dogs. Now we'll have prayers.'

At playtime Fletcher pointed out that he and Bobby had behaved themselves as well as possible, ever since they had sat down in school.

'Only because I half-killed you,' said Ruth. 'I sprained my thumb when I was pinching your neck.'

'But we were good,' said Fletcher.

'Gey good,' said Bobby. 'You promised we could practise sports.'

'After playtime,' said Ruth. 'But everybody's got to keep as good as they were, because we've sent off the postcard.'

'We'll get worse if we don't practise,' said Fletcher.

'Get the things out,' said Ruth. 'I'll help Shirley.'

Shirley was sitting on the kitchen table dipping a stick of rhubarb into the sugar and sucking it, and not really thinking of the job at all. She was looking out of the window at the sky. She blinked at Ruth. 'Have a suck,' she said.

'They're playing rotten old sports,' said Ruth. 'So I'll help you.'

'Good,' said Shirley. 'Why can't you get potatoes already cooked, or with zips on or something like bananas? My thumb gets all wrinkled and chopped at the end.'

'We can always sticking-plaster it,' said Ruth. 'We haven't had to sticking-plaster anyone yet.'

77

'We have now,' said Shirley. Ruth picked up Shirley's hand, which was in the water with the potatoes.

'Stop it,' said Shirley, 'all the water's running down my elbow. It isn't me that's cut, but Betty. She just jumped higher than she could over the bar, and she's cut her knee.'

'Quick,' said Ruth. 'Make a hospital. Put up one of the tables.'

Bobby brought Betty in, and she stood by the door holding her knee whilst Bobby helped to put the table up. Then they made her lie on it whilst they looked at her knee.

'Which one was it?' said Ruth.

'This one,' said Betty, pointing. 'It doesn't hurt any more, though.'

'We'll wash it,' said Ruth. 'I'll get your towel, and wash it with that.'

Shirley brought a bowl of water, and they bathed the knee. It was not an easy job to do tidily. In a little while Betty began to wriggle, because the water was running along the table and getting underneath her. 'I'm lying in it,' she said.

'We're just getting down to your skin,' said Ruth.

'I know,' said Betty.

'Here we are,' said Ruth, using the dry end of the towel to wipe away the last muddy water. 'Here's the wound. Can you see it, Shirley?'

'Just to say,' said Shirley. 'It isn't very big.' She went into the schoolroom and brought back a ruler. 'It's nearly half an inch long,' she said.

'How deep?' said Betty.

'It's about as deep as the groove on a gramophone record,' said Shirley. 'We'll disinfect it, and then sticking-plaster it.'

When they had dabbed and patched the wound Betty went out to jump again. Ruth swabbed up the water on the table and said, 'We never get anything real happening, do we?'

They went back to the last few potatoes.

After dinner there was more playtime. At the end of it Bobby and Fletcher and Peter were missing.

'They went off in the fields,' said Betty. 'They said they'd finished with school.'

'Did they?' said Ruth. 'Well, we'll do something nice whilst they aren't here, and that'll teach them.

The little ones can have the playhouse out in the yard, and we'll all go in the field and I'll read to you, and you can draw at the same time, and I'll give you lots of marks for the drawings, and they won't get any. And you can have a sweet to suck, because there's just enough of them without the boys. That'll cap them.'

It was really a good way to spend the afternoon, because Friday is not a hard-working day. In fact, it was really a sleepy sort of day, and Ruth found herself yawning as she read, and her eyes clouding with the big tears that yawning brings, so that she had to keep shaking her head. Then she found her elbows aching and her breath getting short, because she was lying on her front with the book on the ground. The other side of the wall the little ones were running in and out of their play house at the tops of their voices, and across in the fields the hay was being led in. Ruth was just going to ask one of her pupils to get her the cushion from inside so that she could curl up and relax, when she heard hard shoes running in the yard.

'Ruth,' said Fletcher's voice. 'He's coming. Where are you at? He's just up the road.'

Fletcher looked over the wall. Ruth propped herself up to look at him. She felt like a seal reared up on its flippers.

'The inspector,' said Fletcher. 'We saw him again. He's coming. He didn't see us.'

'Lucky for you,' said Ruth. Then she realized that if the school was going to be inspected it would have to be perfect, with Susan and Bill reading hard words,

and Fletcher doing his fractions perfectly. 'Quick,' she said. 'Everybody inside. Everybody be tidy.'

'Cup of tea,' said Shirley. 'That's what you give people. I'll put on the kettle. I'll fill it with hot water, and it'll be quicker.'

The top class and the middle class climbed the wall into the yard. They took the playhouse down round the little family inside it, and took it in, and shooed the little ones in after it and put them in their desks. Ruth gave them copying of letters to do.

'Arithmetic,' she said. 'Be doing your last lot again. Fletcher, you just copy a good one from Shirley's book, and pretend you've done it. Bobby, do up your shoe. Peter, stop panting like a dog.'

Ruth pulled the arithmetic-with-answers out of the

cupboard and began to do a hard-looking fraction on the board.

There was the noise of a car engine outside. It stopped.

'I'll be explaining this sum,' said Ruth. 'Now, this is three-quarters divided by one-sixth, you see, three over four divided by one over six. Can anyone tell me the special secret about dividing fractions?'

The school door rattled. Someone was trying it. The latch moved. The door began to open. The inspector stood in the doorway. He was wearing his flat-topped blue cap. He had in his hand a book. It would be his complaints book, Ruth thought.

'Here's the tea,' said Shirley, coming through with the teapot. 'Oh, he's here.'

Chapter Twelve

'STAND up, children,' said Ruth. She knew that was the first thing to do when there was a visitor.

'Don't disturb yourselves,' said the man. 'Can I come in?'

'It's perfectly all right,' said Ruth. 'Do come in. Would you care for a cup of tea?'

'Oh,' said the man. 'That'd be grand.'

'There isn't any milk,' said Shirley. 'But there's plenty of sugar.'

'I like it all ways,' said the Inspector. 'But you go on with your lesson. I'll just stay here and sup the tea.'

'Please come and sit down,' said Ruth. 'Class, you can sit down too, if you want, and go on with your work.' Then she spoke to the Inspector again: 'Would you like to take the lesson, and see how the scholars are doing?'

The man smiled. 'My schooling's long done,' he said. 'I don't worry about it now.'

'We'll bring you the books, then,' said Ruth. 'Do you want to see the register, and count the dinner money, and look at the kitchen? And Bill and Susan can nearly read.'

'There's only one thing I want to look at,' said the

man. 'And that's the electricity meter, up here in this box.'

'Oh,' said Ruth. 'But we thought you were an Inspector, and we're all ready to be inspected. We saw you the last time you came, but we had the door locked to stop people walking on the floor because we'd had to wash it.'

'I never thought to knock,' said the man. 'I just thought school must be out for the day. And I am an Inspector, but not a school inspector. I just read the meters.' Now he had the cup of tea that Shirley had poured him. He stirred it with the spoon, felt the cup to see how hot it was, put it down on the window sill, and stepped up beside it to get to the box where he said the meter was. It was the cupboard they had wanted to open but had not been able to. The man brought out a bunch of keys, jingled round it until he found the right one, opened the door, looked carefully into the cupboard, and wrote down something in his notebook. It was not a complaints book, after all.

'That's it,' he said, stepping down again on to the floor, and taking up his cup of tea again. 'Inspected.'

'We'll just go on with our arithmetic,' said Ruth. 'Now, look at this sum, children. Now, what does it mean? It means, how many times does one-sixth go into three-quarters?'

'Heck,' said Fletcher.

'We haven't heard much about Burton school this week,' said Mum, the next day, sitting on Ruth's bed when she brought her her breakfast. 'It can't have been so bad.'

'Oh, school,' said Ruth. 'It's just the same, really.'

'A bit overcrowded, by what you're used to,' said Mum.

'Just about the same as usual,' said Ruth. 'I think I'll have bread and treacle first, and then bacon.'

'Just as you like,' said Mum. 'It's all the same in half an hour.'

'But I'm not thinking of it by then,' said Ruth.

When Ruth was up Mum thought to give her a treat, by letting her cook the dinner by herself. 'You don't get a chance except at the week-end,' she said. 'Your poor old Mum gets tired of it during the week.'

'I know how you feel,' said Ruth. 'I suppose I'd better do it.'

'Good lass,' said Mum. 'I'm going to fetch in some bales, before it drops a shower. It's just demming in for rain now.'

Ruth cooked the dinner. It was no trouble, because it was such a little meal: a handful of potatoes, a mouthful of meat, a shred of cabbage, a cup of custard, and a stick of rhubarb. The amounts weren't really quite so small, but they were hardly measurable against the school cooking.

Fletcher and Bobby were out in the fields all day. They had gone out long before Ruth was awake, and she heard them coming back on a tractor long after she had gone to bed, whilst she was lying awake wondering if this was the night that never got quite dark. She knew there was one, somewhere in the middle of summer. She heard the passing tractor splash water up from its wheels, and Bobby calling good night to

Fletcher. The rain shook the leaves of ivy on the wall, and tinkled in the gutters.

Monday morning was showery still, but the ground was so warm that the rain dried as it fell, steaming up and making knee-high mist between the walls, and filling the fields with a strange crop of cloud. Fletcher came yawning to school, after two late nights and early mornings, and flopped in his desk, quite unable to remember what fractions were. Shirley was teaching, and she had to ask him twice whether he was at school at all. He said he was, in the end, when she threatened to mark him off the register. Shirley said she didn't believe he was quite there this morning.

'I might as well be off, then,' said Fletcher.

'Have you brought a note?' said Shirley. 'No? Then sit down. No, be useful, and clean the board.'

With Fletcher so sleepy, Bobby thought it was his turn to be troublesome. He began by tapping Peter on the head with a ruler, so that Peter had to defend himself. Bobby had to defend himself again, in turn, and in a minute they were having a fight. Fletcher sat down and watched.

Shirley tapped on the desk with the ink bottle. Miss Oldroyd used to do the same. 'Sit down, everyone,' she said. 'I'll be putting you on the list for Miss Oldroyd in a minute.'

'It's his fault,' said Fletcher.

'I don't care how bad you're being naughty,' said Shirley. 'Naughty is bad enough, and I'll take all your names. Open your arithmetic books.'

'We have arithmetic all the week round,' said Bobby. 'Why can't we have something else?'

'What else?' said Shirley. She knew quite well that she taught arithmetic because it was the easiest thing for the teacher, particularly if the answers were in the back of the book. It was much easier than History or Geography, though she knew that Bobby preferred Geography. Now he said that he would rather have a Geography lesson.

'Well,' said Shirley, 'you come and teach it. I'm not very good at Geography. I'll go and help Ruth.'

Bobby grinned and put away his arithmetic book. He came out, picked up the chalk, and stood in front of the class.

'Geography,' he said. 'The geography of England. England is an island. That means it has water all round it, except at the top, where it has Scotland instead.'

Then he stopped. He turned the chalk round in his fingers, and the class looked at him.

'Go on,' said Shirley. She was still in the kitchen doorway.

'We live in England,' said Bobby. 'So I think you know as much about it as I do. Write an essay on it.'

'No, don't,' said Shirley. 'You've got to teach them something before they write about it, and you haven't taught them a thing. Go and sit down, Bobby. It isn't easy to be a teacher, you know.'

'I was only trying,' said Bobby. He put the chalk down by the blackboard, and went to his place.

'Now we'll have a real lesson,' said Shirley. 'We'll do a General Knowledge paper. Fletcher, get the board down for me, and I'll write on the back of it. And whilst I'm doing it you all read about general knowledge so you can get it all right.'

Fletcher put the board behind Miss Oldroyd's desk, and Shirley knelt down to write the questions on it. She made them up as she wrote them. Then she had the board put back, and went to teach the little ones their alphabets whilst the class worked.

Ruth taught the next day. Fletcher was very naughty all the morning. He was so bad that his desk fell over once, and Ruth had to write his name down on the list for Miss Oldroyd. She thought that would cure him of naughtiness, but it only made him worse. He thought he would be getting into trouble in any case, and it wouldn't really matter what he did now. By the end of the afternoon he was on the list again, and had been sent out once. He had had to come in again, because he jumped up and down and looked in the window all the time.

'What are we to do with him?' said Ruth.

'Let him cook,' said Bobby. 'He gets bored of school.'

Chapter Thirteen

'L E T him cook, indeed,' said Ruth. She was answering Bobby, who thought that Fletcher would not be so naughty if he did the cooking. 'Let him stew in his own juice.'

'He *can* cook,' said Bobby.

'Not here he can't,' said Ruth. 'And that's an absolute fact. He can't do the best things just because he's naughty.'

Shirley wondered whether cooking was the best thing. It had an interest the first time, and wasn't too bad the second time, but the third time and the fourth were very tiresome; in fact, the fourth time was so tiresome that it was making her weary already, though she wouldn't have to do it until the day after tomorrow.

'Hm,' she said, meaning all the things she had just thought. Ruth understood what she meant by her remark.

'You must agree it's better than lessons,' she said. 'It's really better than teaching, isn't it?'

'It's nowhere near,' said Shirley. 'I'd rather teach a crocodile than boil a potato.' Then she changed the subject, because an idea was coming to her, and she knew Ruth would never approve it if she heard. 'Let's go and paddle under the bridge.'

'And make mud pies in the sand,' said Ruth, changing the subject almost back to cooking again.

The next morning Fletcher was bad again. He came to school late, and he only came then because he had nothing to do outside in the drizzly day. He did not even have a friend to play with, because Shirley had pulled Bobby all the way to school without letting him free for a minute. Bobby had struggled all the way, and Shirley came into school hot and cross, with rain running down her neck inside. The rain was a bad thing, she thought, because she could not make the boys take the sports practice.

Lessons went quietly for a little while. Fletcher was not marked present in the register. Then the door opened, and Fletcher came tramping in. He took a long time over hanging up his coat. Shirley hoped he would go out again. Perhaps he had decided not to come in after all. But he did come in. He was holding his hands together so that there was a hollow between them.

'What have you got there?' said Shirley. 'Let me see it at once.'

Fletcher stumped across the room, with a great big grin on his face, holding his hands out in front of him. Shirley picked up the ruler. Fletcher opened his hands.

There was a green thing on his fingers. Shirley did not have time to see what it was before it jumped into the air, higher than her head, and landed among the desks, amongst all the good pupils working at their

books. The green thing jumped down, and the whole school jumped up and ran to the other end of the room. The green thing gave a rusty squeak, and jumped again.

Shirley went back behind Miss Oldroyd's desk. 'Take that grasshopper out at once, Fletcher,' she said.

'If I can keep it,' said Fletcher, walking round amongst the desks with his hands cupped in front of him like a fielder in a test match. 'Come on, boy, jump to me.'

'I'll be longstop,' said Bobby, getting behind Fletcher.

'Keep it off us,' said the girls at the other end of the room.

'Go back to your places,' said Shirley. But no one moved. Only Peter came out to help.

'I'm going to get the list out,' said Shirley.

'Oh, aye,' said Fletcher. 'You spell its name Grasshopper. By, it's a good un, it's as fit as a lop, and going like one and all.'

'I spell it Fletcher,' said Shirley. 'And Bobby, and Peter.'

But it was no good. The boys were not listening. Shirley put the names on the list for Miss Oldroyd, and put the list away. She hoped that if she stayed calm and severe that the boys would turn good. They didn't. They grew worse. They began to jump on the desks, like grasshoppers themselves. Fletcher even jumped on to Miss Oldroyd's desk. Then he jumped on top of the cupboard.

'Maybe it's up here,' he said, with his face in the corner of the walls. Shirley took the chair away that he had jumped up from. Fletcher put down his foot so that he could climb on to the chair. He was going to jump up again, if he could.

'Put it back,' he said. 'I can't stop up here.'

Ruth had heard the noise from the kitchen. She did not want to interfere with Shirley's lessons, but she came through with the big wooden spoon. She tapped Bobby on the head, like an egg just boiled, prodded Peter, and then came across and thumped the bits of Fletcher that hung over the cupboard.

'What's all the fuss?' she said.

'A grasshopper,' said Shirley. 'Fletcher brought it in.'

'Ugh,' said Ruth. 'Where is it?'

The grasshopper had walked under the piano, and seemed to be watching everybody who was trying to catch him. Shirley pointed to it. Ruth edged him out with the wooden spoon, then turned her face away and put her hand on him.

'He's strong,' she said. 'He's fighting like anything. Open the door, Shirley.'

The grasshopper went into the hedge the other side

of the road. Ruth came in again, holding her hand away from herself as if it didn't really belong. 'I don't fancy it after that thing's been on it,' she said. 'I don't know how people can pick them up for fun.'

She gave Fletcher, who was still kneeling on the narrow top of the cupboard, another thump; and then put a chair for him to climb down.

'And,' she said, 'we haven't made you any dinner, so you'll be lucky if you get any. We'll leave you till last to be served, and if you don't behave you won't get a thing.'

He was better until dinner time, so they gave him some dinner. After dinner he was very idle. He spent his time making drawings where he should have been doing sums. He was better than he had been, because Ruth was behind him now, with the wooden spoon.

At the end of the day Shirley said: 'I'm going to punish you, Fletcher, with a very hard punishment. Tomorrow. . . .'

'If I come,' said Fletcher.

'Tomorrow you can cook the dinner, and see how you like that,' said Shirley. 'We're tired of you in here.'

'I said,' said Bobby.

'I don't mind that,' said Fletcher. 'But you don't put my name on that list as well, do you?'

'We'll see,' said Shirley.

Fletcher was at school first the next day, going through the kitchen cupboard and tasting everything. He had taken a sniff at the bag of pepper and sneezed so hard that he knocked a wasp out of the air, into the sink, and down the drain. He was trying to lower a

piece of string to it, to let it climb to safety, when Shirley came with the food she had bought.

'It's stew,' she said.

'Aye,' said Fletcher. 'I'll want Bobby.'

'You can have him,' said Shirley. 'And Peter.'

The first thing they did was to rescue the wasp, by using the tea-strainer. Fletcher went outside and put the strainer over the end of the waste pipe and Bobby put the plug in the sink and half-filled it with water. Then he lifted the plug out, and the water washed the wasp through, and Fletcher caught it in the strainer and tapped it out on the window sill to dry. Then they put a chair against the kitchen door, and settled to their cooking.

'I don't know what they'll give us,' said Shirley. 'Shall I take the little ones, and you do the others, Ruth?'

It was a peaceful morning. Nobody ran about and made a fuss or knocked over their desks or jumped on the cupboards. The little ones wrote their figures and letters, and the older ones listened to the wireless, and the sun shone in as quietly as a dream.

At twelve o'clock the kitchen door opened. A cloud of steam came into the room. Fletcher looked into the room. His face was red and shining.

'Set the tables,' he said. 'It's about ready to eat.'

Chapter Fourteen

'WHAT is the dinner? Do you want any help, Fletcher?' said Ruth.

'Just put up the tables,' said Fletcher. 'Then we're ready for you.'

Ruth sniffed at the steam that was pouring from the kitchen. 'It isn't burnt,' she said. Fletcher looked at her severely.

When the tables were up and the places laid, and the jugs of water brought through covered with misty steam, Fletcher brought out a pile of plates.

'You should have served in there,' said Ruth. 'We always did.'

'We warmed up the plates,' said Fletcher.

Ruth put her hand on them. 'You certainly did,' she said. 'I wonder why they didn't melt.'

The plates were very hot. Of course, they were not hot enough to melt, but the bottom one of the pile made an odd noise when Fletcher put them down on the table. He lifted the pile again, and half the bottom plate stopped on the table.

'Never mind,' said Ruth, because she was not going to spoil Fletcher's dinner with little things like broken plates.

'Won't have to,' said Fletcher. 'We put plenty in.'

Bobby came through next, carrying a pan with a lid on. After him was Peter, with another pan, not so big as Bobby's. Bobby's was the one with a big handle and a little one, the pan that held all the potatoes. Fletcher went back to the kitchen and carried something else in. It was a big pie, with a crust on. Bobby helped him lower it on to the table.

'Where did you get that?' said Shirley, bending over it to look at the pastry.

'Made it, what else,' said Fletcher. 'It's siddoned along the edge.'

'It is a bit black,' said Shirley. 'What's in it? Blackbirds?'

Fletcher picked up a knife and a spoon. 'Sixteen of us,' he said. 'There's a fraction to make out of it. I don't frame so well with fractions, so you set out the lines.'

'Cut it across the middle each way,' said Ruth. 'That'll be four. That's right.' The knife went in, and gravy rose up over the edges of the cut. Crumbs fell off the edge on to the table. Bobby picked one up and put it in his mouth. 'Now do the same cut to each quarter,' said Ruth. 'That's it. Now how many is it?'

'Fifteen,' said Fletcher, counting the squares of pastry. 'And one leaf in the middle's got itself sunk.'

The little ones had the middle pieces, because they were thinner and the rest was dished out evenly. 'It's good and thick,' said Fletcher. 'If you get a burnt edge cut it off and leave it.'

Bobby opened up the potato pan. The boys had mashed the potatoes.

'I wish I'd thought of that,' said Ruth. 'But I never

did. I just knew which potato belonged to which person, because they sort of got named when I peeled them.'

The second pan had something green in it. Peter spooned it out on to each plate. Shirley stirred hers with her finger. 'What is it?' she said. 'It looks like boiled grass.'

'Aye,' said Peter. 'It is boiled grass. It's not so good raw.'

'It's no better cooked,' said Shirley, tasting a length. 'But it's no worse. It's better than cabbage.'

'I thought of it,' said Peter. 'It's only leaves, it isn't stalks.'

The dinner was a great success. Even the grass was eaten, and the scorched crust, and every spoonful of gravy and every scraping of potato, and all the water was drunk to wash it down.

'That was the best meal I've ever had,' said Ruth. Fletcher looked pleased with himself.

'There's a pudding,' he said. He took the pie dish out, cold and empty, and came back with a big bowl.

'That's what we wash up in,' said Ruth.

'I scrubbed it,' said Bobby. 'Three times. It was all right before I began, so it must have been perfect when I'd finished.'

The bowl was half full of custard. In the custard there was something green. 'It's a sort of trifle,' said Fletcher. 'I made it up out of this and that.'

'How did you make custard without milk?' said Ruth.

'Went on home for some,' said Fletcher. 'We've got plenty.'

100

He was spooning out the trifle on to the plates. Under the custard with the greenness in it there was a sponge cake, and jam inside the sponge.

'More grass,' said Shirley. 'Or does your cow give green milk?'

'It's apple leaves,' said Fletcher. 'Those leaves that taste like apple. It's an apple flavour trifle.'

Shirley tasted it. 'It's perfect,' she said. 'I mean, it's better than you think, with all leaves in it. Where did you get the cake?'

'It's an old one that never got eaten in the hayfield on Saturday,' said Fletcher. 'It was just in our kitchen. I took it off the dog.'

Shirley put down her spoon. 'You didn't,' she said.

'The dog hadn't had it,' said Fletcher. 'What do you think?'

The trifle disappeared out of the bowl. The bowl was scraped clean. Plates were licked, and everybody sat back.

'I's full,' said Bill. 'Is there any more?'

There was no more. There was only the washing up. Ruth went through to see the kitchen, and knew that the boys would never get it straight after them. She sent them out to play, tied on an apron, and set to work, sweeping all the crumbs and scraps on to the floor, where there was flour and milk and grass mixed already. She worked from the top down, and cleared the kitchen before beginning to wash up. In the end she left the pie dish to soak until next day and went to dry the wrinkles out of her hands in the sunshine of the yard.

The boys were perfect for the rest of the day. Everybody was pleased with them for providing the biggest dinner anyone could remember, and they were so pleased with themselves that they did not need to be naughty.

Before they went into school they put the dustbins outside, and when they had been collected went out and brought them in again, and washed their hands without complaining at all. Ruth had been certain that they would complain about the job, and she had been thinking all day that there would be an argument and that she and Shirley would have to give in and take the bins out themselves.

The next day the boys said they had cooked the only thing they had been able to think of, and that they would rather do easy lessons instead. 'It's all right,' said Ruth. 'It's my turn and I don't mind doing it. But I won't give you grass, if you don't mind.' She gave them shepherd's pie instead, using the pie dish again, and mashing the potatoes to go on top. After it she gave them a fruit salad, with the first strawberries from the garden at home, sliced up bananas, sliced up apple, and a tin of pineapple chunks to sweeten it all. There was no custard.

'It was all right, you know,' said Shirley. 'Nice, and that.' But Ruth knew that no one had been able to eat too much; no one had leaned back and felt they were full to the back teeth. No one had had to make themselves eat the last spoonfuls just because it would be silly to leave them.

'I remember yesterday,' said Betty, looking at Fletcher.

'So do I,' said Ruth. Fletcher was very pleased.

He was pleased enough to be very good all the afternoon. He was so good that Ruth took the list of people to report to Miss Oldroyd and tore it up. 'But don't get upsy,' she said.

'Thank you, Ruth,' said Shirley, who was teaching. 'And now I'll read to you.'

She was busy reading to them, and they were all quiet in the room, when there was a noise they knew outside, a familiar rattle. Shirley stopped, and looked up. 'That. . . .' she said, and everybody knew what she meant, because they had heard it too. She had no time to say any more, because straight away the school door opened, and Miss Oldroyd walked in.

'Well I never,' said Miss Oldroyd. 'And what are you all doing here?'

Chapter Fifteen

EVERYBODY stood up. Miss Oldroyd stepped into the room, and looked about. Ruth wished the school had been perfectly tidy, without any dust, and with the board clean. Shirley came away from the teacher's desk and closed the book she had been reading from.

'What *are* you doing here?' said Miss Oldroyd. 'I thought you had all gone to Burton school.'

No one said anything. Shirley looked at Ruth. Ruth looked at the rest of the class, and then at Miss Oldroyd.

'Haven't you been to Burton school at all?' said Miss Oldroyd.

'No,' said Fletcher. 'It's a spot and all.'

'Did Mrs Tunstall come down here, then?' said Miss Oldroyd. 'Where is she now?'

Ruth put her fingers in the belt of her dress and twisted it. 'We did it ourselves,' she said. 'I taught some days.' She was not going to let Shirley be blamed.

'And I taught the other days,' said Shirley. 'I was teaching now.'

'They were so quiet,' said Miss Oldroyd. 'I thought the school was empty. I was taken aback you know, when I saw you all here. I only came to get some books and see about Monday's lessons. But I don't think you really need me, do you? Can I go away for another month?'

'We thought it would be all right,' said Ruth. 'It was my fault, I thought of it, and I made them come.' She was not sure yet whether they were going to get into trouble for what she had led them to do. Miss Oldroyd had only been talking, without saying so far what she felt. Ruth felt something like crying beginning to make a lump in her throat and prickle behind her eyes. She twisted her fingers very tight in her belt.

'I think you've done very well,' said Miss Oldroyd. 'I see you've even got some new pupils, too.'

The lump in Ruth's throat grew very big indeed, and her eyes suddenly grew very hot. It was because hot tears were filling them. The hot tears began to run down her face, and the lump in her throat melted into a sob. She tried to keep her face straight, but it wrinkled up; and then she was crying properly.

'I sometimes feel like that on a Friday too,' said Miss Oldroyd. 'I generally feel better after I've given our Fletcher a crack, and Bobby and Peter too, as often as not.'

'They've been very good,' said Ruth. 'They made the best dinner we ever had.' She meant to say it in a very calm sort of way, but the words were all tangled with sobs, so that they all came squeaky and jumpy.

'Dinners too,' said Miss Oldroyd. 'Have you made the dinners too?'

'You were away, so Mary Crofts didn't come,' said Shirley. 'She wouldn't, would she?'

'Not if she didn't know,' said Miss Oldroyd. 'There

now, Ruth, sit down and have your cry comfortably, and the rest can go out for a playtime. Is that all right, teacher?'

'Yes,' said Shirley. 'It's about time.'

'Anybody else want a good cry?' said Miss Oldroyd. 'Because I think I'm going to have one.'

'I've got one, but it won't come,' said Shirley.

'Stay and talk to us,' said Miss Oldroyd. She sat down beside Ruth and took out her handkerchief. First she mopped up Ruth's tears. Ruth smelt the scent on the handkerchief, faint and sweet. Then Miss Oldroyd dabbed her own eyes. 'I can't help it,' she said. 'You poor things, taking on a whole school by yourselves. Tell me about everything.'

Ruth picked up her skirt and dried her face on it. Her eyes were feeling much cooler now, and the tears were drying, and the sobs were only coming into her chest and not up into her face.

'We haven't been polite yet,' she said. 'How are you, Miss Oldroyd?'

'I'm very well now, thank you,' said Miss Oldroyd. 'I had a lovely rest, and I'm ready to start again on Monday.'

'Oh, good,' said Ruth. 'I'm glad you're well.'

'We don't mind teaching,' said Shirley. 'But the cooking goes on and on. That's why we let the boys do it.'

'Tell me,' said Miss Oldroyd.

They told her about everything; how they had forgotten about dinner on the first day; how the filter had been left running after the telephone had frightened them; how they thought an inspector had come;

how Fletcher had been naughty and how he had got
his good name back again; how they had filled in the
card for the sports and practised; how they had taught
Bill and Susan their writing.

'It sounds more exciting than ordinary school,' said
Miss Oldroyd.

'Too exciting,' said Ruth. 'And Fletcher still can't
do fractions, and I don't think Bill and Susan can read
yet, so we haven't done what we meant. There's been
such a lot of things all the time.'

'I think you've been very clever,' said Miss Oldroyd.
'And now do you think it's time we brought the others
in?'

'Yes,' said Shirley. 'Then you can see what we've
done.'

They spent the next lesson looking at the books, and showing all the work they had done, the tidy cupboards, the bright kitchen, the rearranged pictures.

'They've learned quite a lot,' said Miss Oldroyd, when she had talked to Bill and Susan. 'Bill can read "Dog".'

'It's the picture he reads,' said Shirley. 'Not the word.'

'It's a start,' said Miss Oldroyd.

'It's a stop, too,' said Shirley. 'It's time school was over.'

Miss Oldroyd stood up, looked at the clock, and then at the class. They all stood up, because they knew what she meant.

'I'm sorry,' she said. 'Shirley's taking the lessons today. She'd better take prayers too. I'm not going to start until Monday.'

'Eyes closed,' said Shirley, and look round to see that all eyes were shut. She looked hard at Ruth, and then even harder at Miss Oldroyd, because they were both watching instead of getting ready to say a prayer. Miss Oldroyd closed her eyes. Ruth closed hers. She knew what had happened, and another lump began to grow in her throat. This time it was not a sob, but a laugh. She was wanting to laugh at Miss Oldroyd for being a good pupil and having to obey the teacher.

Some Other Puffins You Might Enjoy

A BOOK OF HEROES
edited by William Mayne

Here are all sorts of heroes and all kinds of heroism gathered together from all the corners of the globe. Some of the heroes are familiar. There is Orlando, whose exploits at the Battle of Roncesvalles were sung at the Battle of Hastings in 1066. There is a fleet of sea heroes – Sir Francis Drake, Sir Richard Grenville, John Paul Jones. But there are also many less known stories, like the one about Kagssagssuk, the homeless Eskimo boy who became so strong he could wring a bear's neck with his bare hands. Or the one about Volund the crippled smith tricking wicked King Nidud.

For readers of eight to twelve.

A HANDFUL OF THIEVES
Nina Bawden

Sid believed that Mr Gribble was sinister the very first time he saw him flapping down Station Road in his big, baggy mackintosh. It was something to do with his thin, sad face and his rich, fat voice. But Fred thought his Gran's new lodger was strange because of his extraordinary diet of Hubbel's Fluid, which tasted remarkably like fish glue.

But both Fred and Sid had more important things to think about anyway. There was the Cemetery Committee. Then there was the Fireworks Fund, which they kept hidden in the wreck of an old Humber saloon. But after the firework party at Gran's, which went suddenly and splendidly right, everything went horribly wrong. All Gran's savings disappeared, together with the mysterious Mr Gribble. In true Committee style, Fred and his friends decided to track down the thief and rescue the stolen savings single-handed.

For ages nine to twelve, boys and girls.

THE TOWN THAT WENT SOUTH
Clive King

Gargoyle the rectory cat made the Discovery on his way to his night hunting grounds; where there should have been railway lines there was only cold, choppy water. Gargoyle went straight to the Vicar, who rang the church bells for everyone to gather in the square and decide what to do about The Flood.

But it wasn't a Flood. It was something even more astonishing. The town of Ramsly had come adrift from the rest of England and was floating gently across the Channel to France. By the author of *Stig of the Dump*.

For readers of eight and over.

THURSDAY RIDES AGAIN
Michael Bond

Thursday the mouse, Michael Bond's new character, reappears as lively and ingenious as ever, and still as accident-prone, together with Mr and Mrs Peck and their nineteen alphabetically-named children. This is a story that will delight all his old readers and make many new converts.

Thursday and the Pecks were tricked into a boat trip to France, when all they had wanted was a ride round the harbour. Something dark and dangerous was going on, and who could say whether they would ever see their peaceful home at St Mary's in the Valley again?

For readers of eight and over.